Penny Bear's
Gift of Love

Penny Bear's
Gift of Love

By Penny Wigglesworth

Illustrated by Michiko Eager

Published By:

Penny Bear Publishing,

The Penny Bear™ Company, Inc.

Marblehead, Massachusetts

The Penny Bear™ Company is a non-profit, all-volunteer organization that
believes in joining hands and hearts with other non-profit organizations to
make a meaningful difference in our world.

(781) 639-2828

www.pennybear.org

ISBN 1-893356-01-9

Library of Congress Control Number: 2003095731

Editing, design, layout, and production provided by:

Quality of Life Publishing Co., Naples, Florida, which specializes in clinical and grief support publications for
hospices and other end-of-life care organizations. Visit **www.QoLpublishing.com** or call **1-877-513-0099** (toll-free
in U.S. and Canada) to learn about grief books and booklets, including *Heart-Shaped Pickles, Afterglow: Signs of
Continued Love, Afterglow for Bereaved Families,* and *Timmy's Christmas Surprise.*

Printed in the **United States of America** by **Four Star Printing Co., Inc.,** Lynn, Massachusetts

I dedicate this book in loving memory of my husband, Giff, who was the shining light in my life and my best friend. Giff truly was the "Big Bear," who supported my dream of writing a story that could help people, especially children, find their way through the grieving process. Throughout our lifetime together, I was blessed to receive the greatest gift of all…Giff's love. Our four children, eight grandsons and I know that he will always be in our hearts. We will treasure our wonderful memories of Giff forever.

— Penny Wigglesworth ♥

CONTENTS

A Welcome Hug

I wrote *Penny Bear's Gift of Love* in honor of Alison Faria and in memory of Seth Bailey, two young friends I grew to deeply love and respect through my relationships with them as a Hospice volunteer.

Alison was eight years old when her Daddy died. As her family's Hospice volunteer, I often listened to Alison's feelings of sadness and loneliness, sometimes anger and confusion. We decided that I should write a book to help her and others understand the many emotions experienced during the grieving process. I was honored by Alison's trust as a child, and I am delighted that years later she and her mother, Linda, remain a part of my life.

Seth Bailey was 16 years old when he came into my life. He was diagnosed with leukemia at age three, underwent a bone marrow transplant at age seven, and needed a double lung transplant to survive. During the time we shared together, Seth learned the importance of discovering a sense of purpose in life. He wanted to find ways to return the love and support he had received from his family and friends.

We talked a lot about our hopes and dreams, and together we

decided to create a non-profit
Penny Bear organization, with
Seth as our first Vice President! I
opened my home so that friends
who believed as we did could help
us establish a workshop for volunteers. We began with a single

project: sending messages of love, hope, trust, and compassion
out into the world through one of the most universal ambassa-
dors — the teddy bear.

Through his gentle, giving spirit, Seth taught all of us about
courage, love, and helping others. In my heart, I know Seth is
happy that "his" idea for sharing love through the Penny Bears
became a reality, and I continue to quietly thank him in my prayers.

All of us involved in the loving outreach of the Penny Bear
volunteers hope you enjoy *Penny Bear's Gift of Love.* Written from
my heart, it is a story about a sad little boy named Johnathan and
a magical bear who comes into his life just when he needs a very
special friend. We hope that the story, told by the little bear known
as "Penny Bear," touches your heart in gentle ways.

— Penny Wigglesworth ♥

January

Hello! I'm Penny Bear. To many people, I'm just an ordinary teddy bear, cute and cuddly. But to you and Johnathan Clarke, I'm magical. Johnathan is a wonderful young boy who's very sad because his mom died. I came into Johnathan's life just when he needed me most. Here's my story of our very special friendship.

As I peeked over the staircase railing into the living room, I could see Johnathan and his dad still hugging each other goodnight. They just didn't want to let one another go. Johnathan's dad put on a brave smile, and Johnathan tried to do the same. It had been the hardest day of their lives.

A lot of people had come to his mom's funeral. Many had kissed and hugged him, even people he didn't know. Some of the women wore so much perfume that it gave him a head-ache. He was relieved the day was over and glad everyone had finally gone home. My bear heart felt sad as I watched him head for bed, dragging his feet along. It looked as if he were climbing a mountain instead of just the living room stairs.

Johnathan was one tired, unhappy little boy who didn't even see me waiting for him when he flopped on top of his bed — clothes and all. Then his hand brushed the top of my head. "What's this?" he said, sitting up and holding me in his lap. He found the tag on my arm and started to read it out loud:

> *Hello! I'm Penny Bear...*
>
> *I am named "Penny Bear" because I carry a shiny penny in my rainbow heart pocket with the message..."In God We Trust."*
>
> *I'm here to be your new friend when you're feeling happy or sad. Together we can share smiles, plenty of hugs, secrets, and lots of love...*

Johnathan stopped reading and gave me a big hug. "I'm so glad you're here, little Penny Bear," he said. "I sure do need lots of hugs." His eyes filled with tears as he added, "But mostly I just want my mom back!" I did everything in my bear power not to talk out loud just then. I'm supposed to go slowly and not show off my magical talents until the time is right.

Not long after Johnathan had changed into his pajamas and climbed into bed, I thought he had fallen asleep. Instead, he was whispering wishes and making promises. "I wish my mom would come back and be my mom again. I promise I'll be a much better kid. I won't be so noisy, and I won't leave my

sneakers in the living room any more. I'll even help with the dishes, and I'll never..." Well, his list was as long as a giraffe's neck, and he fell asleep in the middle of another promise. I snuggled close to him. I needed my "bear sleep," so I could be ready to help him in the morning when he woke and realized his mom wouldn't be there.

Sunlight poured in through the bedroom window the next

morning as we both woke up. Johnathan rubbed his eyes and said, "Hi, Penny Bear. Did you sleep, too?" I knew he didn't really expect an answer. Then his face changed and he started to cry as he remembered that his mom wasn't there. "Why did she have to die, Penny Bear?" he said, turning and pushing his face into the pillow. "I loved her so much! Why? Why? Why? It's not fair! It's not fair." He pulled me to him and hugged me hard for several minutes, and I could feel his sad heart pounding.

Then Johnathan sat up and wiped his tears with the back of one hand, still holding my paw with the other. He looked at my tag and decided to finish what he had been too tired to read last night. Slowly he read:

"It's okay not to have the answers to all of your questions... some will come in time, and some will always remain a mystery. I'm a good listener, and I'll always be nearby to hear the whispers of your heart. When you just need a cuddle and the warmth of a hug, I'll always be near to give you my love. Your friend forever, Penny Bear."

He looked at me sadly and said in a quiet voice, "I don't think I'll ever be happy again without my mom." Then with a big sigh he added, "Well, Penny Bear, I'm glad you're here to be my new friend."

Just as I finally felt ready to speak, Mr. Clarke came into the room to tell Johnathan it was time to get ready for school. "Daddy, can't I stay home today?" Johnathan said, lying back down and pulling the covers up to his chin. "I just want to stay in bed forever and not go to school or anywhere else."

Mr. Clarke sat down on the bed. "I know, son," he said, squeezing Johnathan's shoulder gently. "I don't want to go to my office today, either, but it's what I have to do. I'm going to go in and try to have as normal a day as possible and I want you to do the same." He pulled Johnathan up into a hug. "So," he said, "let's both use our 'I'll try' attitudes and get through the day the best we can, okay?" Johnathan leaned against his dad and nodded slowly. Then he dragged himself out of bed and got dressed for school. I knew how hard it was for him to even put one foot in front of the other to walk.

As Johnathan started down the stairs for breakfast, I wanted to call out to him, "Hey, wait! What about me?!" Because I'm magical, I can always tell what he's thinking, but this time he must have read *my* mind, because he came back to get me.

Johnathan didn't eat much breakfast. He just pushed the cereal around and around in the bowl and let his toast get

cold on the plate. "Come on, Penny Bear," he said as he cleared
the table. "I guess if I have to go to school, you'll have to
come with me." He stuffed me into his backpack and we
headed for school, just two blocks away.

Johnathan's teacher, Miss Nancy, sat on the steps of the school, greeting each boy and girl as they arrived. When she saw Johnathan, she came over to him, put her arm around his shoulder, and said in a choked-up voice that she was so sorry that his mom had died.

Johnathan didn't know what to say because he had never seen a teacher cry before. So he just shrugged his shoulders as they walked into the building together. As they passed two other teachers, Johnathan heard one of them whisper, "Poor child." It made him feel very strange and lonely to be whispered about.

From the moment Johnathan walked into the classroom, everything seemed wrong to him. Even his classmates seemed different. He put his backpack on the floor under his desk with me still squished inside. When it was time for recess, Johnathan pulled me out of his backpack and we went outside to the playground. Johnathan's friends seemed to ignore him. I knew why, but poor Johnathan didn't understand at all. He thought the kids were mad at him, as if he had done something wrong. Johnathan felt left out and lonelier than ever.

Finally, a boy with a ball under his arm came over to Johnathan, and I thought things would be better.

"Hey, Johnathan, wanna play?"

"Nah," Johnathan answered, "I don't feel like it."

"But you're our best kicker," the boy said. "What's wrong with you today, anyway?"

Johnathan dropped his head and said softly, "Nothing, I just don't want to play, okay? Just leave me alone."

The boy turned and walked away. Johnathan could hear another boy say, "Didn't you know his mom's been sick and she died?" The subject ended quickly as the kids got into a lively game of kickball. Johnathan hung his head down even lower and shuffled his feet on the pavement. He wanted to disappear. He wished this day would hurry up and end. I wanted to tell his friends that when someone you love dies, that's the time when you need your friends the most.

The school day finally ended, but I could tell Johnathan wasn't in any hurry to get home, either. For the first time in his life, his mother wouldn't be there to  meet him. Instead, a neighbor named Mrs. Short would stay with him until Mr. Clarke got home. As we walked in the front door, Mrs. Short handed Johnathan a plate of her homemade chocolate chip cookies — his favorite. Johnathan forced a smile and a quiet "thank you" and took the plate of warm cookies out to the kitchen table. After Mrs. Short went downstairs to do some laundry, Johnathan turned to me and said, "Even these cookies taste yucky. Nothing's ever going to be the same again without Mom!"

He grabbed me and ran into the living room, where he flopped into a comfortable chair in the corner. He fell asleep and didn't wake up until Mr. Clarke came home. At supper time, neither Johnathan nor his dad had much to say. Both of them looked pretty tired. Their first day of trying to do "normal" things like going back to work and school had taken every bit of energy they had.

When Johnathan climbed into bed that night, he told me how much he hated school and that he was never going back. I listened as he went on about how he hated his friends, too, and how awful everyone and everything was. "I'm never going to eat again, either. I'm going to stay in bed until it's time for *me* to die, too. No one will care anyway!"

Johnathan cried so hard that I knew I couldn't stand it any longer. It was time to use my magic. I cleared my throat, and the words that came out sounded sort of scratchy. "It's okay, Johnathan, you can tell me anything you want. You know, I will listen to you with my whole heart." From the way Johnathan's face lit up with surprise, I knew it didn't matter *how* I sounded.

"I knew it! I knew it! You have magic! I just knew you could talk, Penny Bear!" Johnathan exclaimed.

He asked me all about myself, and I told him lots of stuff, including the fact that I came from a long line of ancestors.

"It was my great-great grandfather who invented the 'bear hug,' Johnathan. That was shortened later to just the word 'hug.' You see, when you hug someone, it means that you care about them without having to say anything. My grandfather taught me that hugs help us share love, and I'm proud to carry his message to everyone everywhere."

He asked me question after question about what it's like to be a magical bear, and I talked and talked until my mouth was dry. Then I reminded him that part of my job was to be a good listener, and it was *his* turn to talk.

Johnathan told me he had so many feelings stuck way down in his stomach that he thought he might pop like a balloon. "That's exactly why I brought you a calendar, so you can write down those 'feeling words' in the little squares on each page," I said. You'll find it in the bag I came in, under the tissue paper." Johnathan pulled out the calendar and flipped through the pages. He liked the drawings of my relatives, friends, and — of course — me, too. "This is a cool calendar," he said, "but what are 'feeling words'?"

I explained that whenever he had a feeling inside that seemed to be stuck and made his stomach hurt, he could write down a word or two that would describe that feeling. Johnathan reached for a pencil from his bedside table and wrote down "yucky, sad," and "mad at my friends." He even wrote, "mad at my mom." He looked at me for a reaction, especially to those last words. I gave him a hug and told him that everything he had written were his feelings, and that they came from his heart. They weren't right or wrong, good or bad. "It's very important to try to write down whatever you are really feeling, Johnathan. It's better than keeping everything stuffed inside."

I also explained to Johnathan that his friends acted the way they did at school because they didn't know what to say to him. They were sad that his mom had died. They wanted to help him feel better but didn't know how, so they just stayed away. "I think I understand, Penny Bear, but they really hurt my feelings and made me feel left out of everything. And that made me feel lonely."

Johnathan decided to add more words to his calendar, so he wrote, "left out, hurt, lonely." Then he looked at me again. "You really know how to listen to me about the stuff I feel, Penny Bear." Then he reached over and gave me the best hug ever. And a little while later, we drifted off to sleep. ♥

FEBRUARY

Of course, Johnathan did go back to school, and some things got easier and more comfortable for him as time went on. But some things got harder.

When he turned the calendar page to February, I could see that Johnathan was having a hard time. Everywhere he looked, he was forced to think about Valentine's Day. When he went shopping with his dad or Mrs. Short, he'd see decorations, cards, and all sorts of heart-shaped things. When he watched television, he'd hear announcers talk about ordering candy or flowers "for that special someone." And in Johnathan's school, the classrooms were decorated with hearts and cupids, and the teachers were busy planning Valentine's Day projects.

A few weeks earlier, I had suggested to Johnathan that we begin a special routine at bedtime. We decided to have "boy-to-bear" talks and take turns sharing our ideas, plans, thoughts, feelings, or just plain old silliness.

One night in February, Johnathan asked for a boy-to-bear talk. He had a lot on his mind. He told me he was feeling sad for his dad, because Valentine's Day was such a special time in their family. "Last year, and every year before then that I can remember, Dad brought Mom home a huge bunch of roses — big red ones. She always seemed surprised, and she always gave him a big hug and a kiss."

I snuggled closer to him, listening. "And then Mom would smile and cry at the same time when she read her Valentine's Day cards from Dad and me. Last year I asked her why she was crying when she was happy, and she told me about 'happy tears.' She bent down so I could see the tears rolling down her cheeks. She told me to look really close, because if a teardrop sparkled, that meant that it wasn't a sad tear, it was a teardrop full of love and happiness. And I saw them on her face — I saw her happy tears."

Johnathan got very quiet. So we just lay there for awhile until we fell asleep.

The next day at school was one of Johnathan's hardest days since I came to live with him. The boys and girls were making Valentine's Day cards for their parents and friends. I could see Johnathan's face begin to scrunch up as he wondered what to do. He knew he could make some cards for his dad and his friends, but the thought of not making one for his mom made him wonder what he was doing all of it for anyway. I saw tears trickle down his face. And not one of them had a sparkle inside. I knew he was hurting — big-time!

Anna was a girl in his class who had blonde curls and a fast way of talking. Today she kept trying to get Johnathan's attention. He liked Anna okay, but some days she could be really annoying. And today was one of those days. Anna kept trying to talk to him and waving her card in the air. She was really bugging him, and he wished she would just leave him alone. When Anna jumped up and ran over to his desk, Johnathan couldn't take it any longer. He gave her a little push that was just enough to make her lose her balance. Anna fell down and started to cry! When Miss Nancy came over to them, Johnathan told her that Anna's card was stupid and that the whole idea of Valentine's Day was *really* stupid.

After Miss Nancy got Anna and the rest of the children settled down, she very gently put her arm around Johnathan's shoulders and asked if he would help her carry some craft supplies from the closet in the next room. Johnathan couldn't wait to get out of the classroom. He grabbed me by the foot, and off we went.

As she lifted down boxes of markers and construction paper from the shelves and handed them to Johnathan, Miss Nancy told him she understood how he was feeling about his first Valentine's Day without his mom. "My dad died when I was your age, Johnathan, and it was really, really hard for me, especially when a holiday or special occasion came along." Johnathan saw a tear or two fall from her eyes. He looked closely, but there was no sparkle in them. "I'm sorry about your dad," he whispered. Miss Nancy gave him a quick hug, and the three of us returned to the classroom.

Johnathan seemed to feel better after that. Maybe it was because he knew that someone else understood what it felt like to be in his shoes. He got busy making Valentine cards. One was so special that he covered it so nobody could see — not even me — while he drew the last pictures on the cover.

When school was over, Johnathan stuffed me into his backpack and headed for home. As he turned the first corner, he heard Anna calling his name. She was running to catch up with us! Johnathan was too embarrassed to say he was sorry for pushing her down. The words just wouldn't come out. But Anna didn't seem upset with him. She walked along with us, talking about her grandmother who had just died. Anna kept using a strange word — "heimgang."

"Wait a minute, Anna," said Johnathan. "what does 'heimgang' mean?" Anna said it was a German word that her grandfather used when he talked about her grandmother's death. It meant "going home."

When we reached Anna's house, she turned and asked, "Are you still mad at me, Johnathan?" He shook his head no,

and with a little wave to her, continued walking to his house.

Once inside, Johnathan put his dad's card on the table by the phone so he would see it the minute he came home. Then he turned to me and asked sadly, "Now what do I do with Mom's Valentine card, Penny Bear?"

I said, "Well, you could make a 'memory box,' where you can keep your card and other special things that remind you of your mom." Johnathan thought it was a great idea. He went down to the work area in the basement and found an old shoe box, glue, and some crayons. After working for a while, he left the box on his dad's workbench, then disappeared for a few minutes. I began to wonder if he'd forgotten about me, but he came back down and showed me a pretty heart-shaped pin he had made for his mother last year. "Mom always said it was her favorite piece of jewelry," he said, "and I want it to be the first special thing in the memory box." As he held up the pin, Johnathan smiled and said, "You know, Penny Bear, I remember how happy Mom looked whenever she wore this." It was a happy memory, and Johnathan felt better just thinking about it.

Then Johnathan showed me the Valentine he had made for his mom. In the center of a bright red heart, Johnathan had pasted his favorite picture of his mom and dad together, with him in the middle. Everyone was laughing, and they looked so happy. Under the picture, Johnathan had written, "For Mom. Here's our picture so you won't forget us. Happy Valentine's Day! Love, Johnathan." As he stared at the picture, I heard him whisper the word, "heimgang." He turned to me and asked, "Do you think my mom has sort of gone home, Penny Bear?" His question touched my heart. I answered, "Johnathan, I think anything's possible. Lots of people believe that when we die, we go to another place that's like home. I don't know for sure, but it's a nice thought, isn't it?" Johnathan gently laid the card in the box.

When it was time for Johnathan and Mr. Clarke to exchange Valentine's Day cards, they hugged and hugged. On the card he made for his dad, Johnathan had drawn a vase of big, beautiful, red roses — just like the ones his dad used to give his mom. And the card Mr. Clarke gave Johnathan was really special. The words written on it said how much he loved

Johnathan and how proud he was to have him as his son. As they hugged one another, I'm sure I saw sparkly tears on both their faces.

It wasn't until later that night, when we were getting ready for bed, that Johnathan showed me his secret card, the one he wouldn't let anyone else see while he was making it. I had "bear tears" myself when I saw that it was for me! It was my very first Valentine. Johnathan could see how pleased I was. Later, I smiled to myself when I noticed that he had tucked the new memory box under his bed. It had turned out to be a very special Valentine's Day for everyone, after all. ♥

MARCH

Sometimes just getting through a regular day was hard enough for Johnathan, and now he was about to face his first birthday without his mom. He worried over which friends to invite to his party. Last year he had asked everyone in his class, but this year, even though his birthday fell on a Saturday, he wished he could just skip the whole thing.

At Mr. Clarke's suggestion, though, Johnathan went ahead and sent invitations to all of his classmates for a Saturday afternoon party. To his surprise, every single kid in his class planned to show up. This made Johnathan feel kind of happy, but it also made him feel pretty nervous. He didn't like the idea of being the center of everyone's attention.

On the morning of his birthday, the March sun shone brightly through the bedroom window. But Johnathan scrunched down and pulled the bed quilt over his head. "I wish this day would just go away, Penny Bear," he said. "I'm going to pretend I'm sick. I'll tell Dad I can't get out of bed, and you can wake me up when it's all over." He started to cry.

"No dumb old birthday is ever going to be any fun without Mom, anyway."

I waited patiently, and my heart ached for him. But I was glad that Johnathan was letting out some of his stuck feelings. When his crying stopped, I climbed up beside him and said, "Johnathan, I understand that you feel your birthdays will never be the same again, and in a way, you're right. They won't be the same as when your mom was here. But maybe we can make this into a *different* kind of birthday party." That got his attention. He peeked out from under his quilt and listened while I explained my plan. Then his frown turned into a grin, and he sat up and said, "Well, Penny Bear, I guess we can give it a try." So he got up and dressed for the big day.

As his friends started arriving that afternoon, Johnathan felt a little strange at first. But then he slowly began to join in the games. Instead of candles, Johnathan and his dad had set one really big sparkler in the center of the birthday cake on the table. It was in memory of his mom, who had loved fireworks. When the games ended, Johnathan lit the sparkler himself, while his dad stood nearby. At that moment, Johnathan felt that his mom was right there with them, and

he smiled happily in the bright glow of the sparkler.

After the cake and ice cream, the "different" part of the party began. Johnathan gave each of his classmates a make-your-own-kite kit. Everyone drew designs or wrote special words on the paper part of their kites. I peeked at Johnathan's yellow kite and saw that he had printed, "I love you, Mom." Then he drew lots of hearts all around the words.

Mr. Clarke led all of the kids up to the top of the hill behind Johnathan's house and showed them how to fly their kites. It didn't take long before the breezes lifted each decorated kite high into the air. The children "oohed" and "aahed" as the kites dipped and sailed against the bright blue sky. Then one of Johnathan's friends called out, "Hey, look! We made a kite rainbow!" Sure enough, the colors of their kites did look like a rainbow. Johnathan whispered to me, "Good plan, Penny Bear. I'll bet Mom really likes what we did." And I had to agree.

When the fun day was finally over, Johnathan and I settled down on the bed to have one of our boy-to-bear talks. Johnathan was all smiles as he told me that his birthday party had been one of his best ever. "It was a lot more fun than staying in bed all day," he said with a silly grin. Then he gave me a hug. "Thanks for saving the day, Penny Bear." ♥

APRIL

The days and weeks that followed seemed like a rollercoaster ride. Johnathan felt "up" some days, and I noticed these were usually the days when he kept busy learning something new at school or practicing his throws and catches with the mitt his dad had given him for his birthday. Other days he felt "down," and today was definitely a down day.

Johnathan was sitting in his tree house in the back yard. He called this big tree his "elephant tree," because the bottom part looked exactly like an elephant's foot, and one of the branches looked like an elephant's trunk. It was really a beautiful old tree, and Johnathan always felt safe when he climbed into it.

There had been many days lately when Johnathan lay on the floor of his tree house watching the clouds float by and wishing that his mom would come back. While he was daydreaming, he reached into his jeans pocket for some bubble gum. His fingers felt the smoothness of my special penny, which he had been carrying with him since I first arrived.

But when he tried to pull out the gum, out fell the shiny penny, bouncing brightly from branch to branch until it landed somewhere below.

Johnathan scrambled down the tree and began crawling through the thick grass, frantically looking for the penny. But he couldn't find it anywhere. I watched from the window as he ran into the house so no one would see that he was crying.

While he tried to catch his breath and tell me what had happened, Johnathan kept saying over and over, "I *hate* losing things! And I *hate* losing my mom!" We hugged for a while and then I told him the first important lesson. "Johnathan, we never really lose those we love, because we always keep them right here in our hearts." I thought Johnathan understood what I meant, but he cried even harder. I was confused.

Johnathan buried his face in my fur and said, "But I never got a chance to say goodbye to Mom the day she died." I gave him a big hug and told him the second important lesson. "Johnathan, when you love someone and they love you back, there are no real goodbyes."

He wiped tears from his cheeks and tried to smile. "I feel like such a baby because I cry all the time."

"It's okay to cry, Johnathan," I said. "In fact, it's good to cry because the tears help wash away some of those stuck feelings we've talked about."

Johnathan took me with him out to the backyard where we searched in the grass for the lost penny. He was getting more and more discouraged, and I suggested he choose another penny from his piggy bank to be his favorite penny. "After all, Johnathan, *every* penny is special," I said, "because each one has those important words on it, 'In God We Trust.'"

I could tell he was only half listening. Suddenly, he spotted the flash of something twinkling in the bark at the foot of the elephant tree. Could it be? Yes! It was the penny!

Johnathan held me by my paws and we danced around in circles. He was so excited and happy that he hugged the tree. Then we *both* hugged the tree. Johnathan giggled and said he felt a little silly hugging a tree, and he hoped no one could see him.

But you know, it felt good, almost as if we were being hugged back. And who knows? ...maybe we were. ♥

May

One Saturday morning at the breakfast table, Johnathan was quieter than usual. He and his dad ate their blueberry pancakes in silence for awhile. Then Mr. Clarke looked up from his newspaper and asked, "Johnathan, is something bothering you that you'd like to talk about?"

Johnathan's eyes suddenly filled with tears and his throat seemed to close up. He blinked and shifted around in his chair for a minute, and then asked, "Dad, are we going to do something special for Mother's Day this year?"

His dad folded the paper and set it aside. "Hmm. I haven't really given it much thought."

Johnathan quickly said, "Well, I have an idea! I hope you don't think it's silly, but maybe, well, maybe we can finish the herb garden that Mom started before she got sick."

Mr. Clarke got up and went around to Johnathan's side of the table. He crouched down so he was eye level with his son. "I think that's a wonderful idea, Johnathan," he said quietly. Then he gave Johnathan a big hug. They began making plans for the garden right away, and Johnathan was more excited than I had seen him in days.

I sat outside on the bench under Johnathan's elephant tree and watched while he and his dad dug in the garden. They planted all of his mom's favorite herbs — the ones that smelled good, the ones that looked pretty, and the ones she had used for cooking. They were almost finished when Johnathan remembered the one plant they had completely forgotten. And it was his mom's favorite of all — lavender!

He and his dad headed for the garden store, and I curled up on the bench for an afternoon nap. When they returned, Mr. Clarke went inside to fix supper, and Johnathan came and sat beside me. I could tell by the way he hunched over and hid his face in his hands that something was very wrong. Then he looked over at me, and I gave him one of those encouraging looks, the kind that lets him know I'm ready to listen.

"When Dad and I got near the lavender plants, the smell made me think about Mom, and I started to cry, right there in the store in front of everybody!" He began pounding on one knee with his fist. "I was so embarrassed I ran outside,

Penny Bear. I felt like such a baby."

I cleared my throat and explained that what he'd had was a "reminder." Johnathan stopped pounding his knee and gave me a look that seemed to say, "what in the world are you talking about?"

"A reminder," I continued, "is something that makes you think about someone you love. Reminders can be songs, or places, or, just like today, a familiar smell." Johnathan told me how some nights when he couldn't sleep, his mom used to put a drop of lavender oil on his pillow and rub his head softly until he fell asleep. The smell in the garden shop had suddenly brought all of that back to him.

"Sometimes reminders sneak up on us when we least expect them," I explained. "Reminders can make us feel sad, but sometimes they make us feel happy and help us to laugh again."

Johnathan was quiet for several minutes. Then his face brightened. "Speaking of happy reminders, Penny Bear, I have a surprise." He reached under the bench and asked me to close my eyes and hold out my paws. What he put into my paws was big and heavy. "Okay, open your eyes. See? It's for Mom. But really it's

for *all* of us."

I was looking down at a big, beautiful rock. Carved into the stone, in bold capital letters, was the word, "LOVE."

"When I saw the rock at the garden shop, I thought about your great-great grandfather and what he said about hugs and loving people," said Johnathan in an excited voice. "And since we made our herb garden with love in memory of Mom, I thought the rock would be perfect. What do *you* think?" I was so moved, I couldn't speak, which is unusual for me.

So Johnathan and I got up and placed the rock carefully in the garden, and he was right — it looked just perfect! ♥

JUNE

A month went by and Johnathan was worrying about the next holiday, Father's Day. He spent many hours thinking about what to give his dad. He wanted to find a Father's Day present that would be so special that his dad would smile all day long.

"Daddy just doesn't seem the same anymore, Penny Bear. I miss how he used to laugh and joke around and do fun things with me," Johnathan said in a sad voice. "Sometimes it feels like I've lost my dad, too." When I heard him say that, I knew it was time for a bear-to-boy talk.

Sometimes when Johnathan and I talked, he would say things like: "Dads are strong...they don't cry. I think my dad forgets he still has me." I tried to explain to Johnathan that his dad was very sad and he needed to feel better, too. "Everyone heals in their own way in their own time, Johnathan."

"I just wish I had a magic wand to make him feel better right now, especially in time for Father's Day." Just after he said that, Johnathan's face looked as if someone had shined a

light bulb on it. "Hey, Penny Bear, I've got a terrific idea! Let's invite Daddy to a picnic to celebrate Father's Day!" Johnathan started to work on a handmade card for his dad, and I was proud to see that he had drawn a picture of me and called his surprise a "Penny Bear Picnic."

When Father's Day finally arrived, Johnathan couldn't wait a minute longer! Wearing a big grin on his face, he handed his dad the card. As Mr. Clarke read it, his eyes filled with tears. Johnathan started to feel uncomfortable, but then he must have remembered our talk about how grownups cry sometimes, too. He went over and hugged his dad. Mr. Clarke smiled down at Johnathan and said, "A picnic! What a great idea!"

We left to go on our picnic around noon. After walking for quite awhile, we came to Johnathan's secret place in the woods. The three of us sat down on a picnic blanket in the warm sunshine and listened to the leaves rustling in the wind. All around us the birds were singing, and the squirrels were happily chasing each other up and down the trees. It certainly *was* a magical place!

When they had both finished the peanut butter and jelly sandwiches Johnathan had packed, he leaned closer to his dad. "Daddy, I don't want to spoil our picnic or anything, but I need to ask you something."

His dad put his arm around Johnathan and replied, "It's a perfect time, so ask away." Johnathan took two deep breaths, and the words came pouring out.

"Why did Mom have to die? Did I do something wrong? Will she ever forget us? Will we forget her? And what if something happened to you, Dad? Who would take care of me?" I sat on the picnic blanket listening to all his difficult questions and understood how much Johnathan hurt inside.

"Johnathan, I've been struggling with lots of 'why' questions, too. It's hard to make any sense out of something so sad. Maybe we will in time, but for now let's remember we have each other. Maybe together we can find some kind of meaning in everything that's happened. But it's really important that you know you didn't do anything wrong. And no, Mom would never forget us. She loved us too much for that to ever happen. And we'll never forget her, either, because we'll keep her right *here* in our hearts."

Johnathan looked over at me, remembering that I had said those same words. It was good to hear them again, especially from his dad.

"I'm sorry about not spending more time with you, Johnathan," Mr. Clarke said. "I'll try to change that. As far as anything happening to me, I'm healthy and I'll do my best to stay that way. If for any reason I couldn't be here to take care of you, you would go live with Aunt Sally and Uncle Doug."

Johnathan felt better hearing that because he knew his aunt and uncle loved him very much, and that they would take good care of him.

Johnathan and Mr. Clarke hugged a lot, cried a little, and they were even able to laugh together, something they hadn't done in a long time. Now that Johnathan had answers to some of his questions, he felt relieved, because he didn't need to think and worry about them so much.

Johnathan looked over at me and gave me a big wink and the thumbs-up sign. I did the same thing back to him. Yes, it was a magical day!

A couple of days after the picnic, while Johnathan and his dad were pulling weeds in the herb garden, Mr. Clarke said, "Johnathan, I've heard that Hospice is going to sponsor a special weekend at a camp in July. It's for people like us — kids and their families who have had someone they love die. I thought you and I could go together. We'd even have our own cabin. What do you think?"

Johnathan thought back to the days when the Hospice nurses and volunteers had come to visit his mom at home while she was sick. He liked the Hospice helpers. They were very nice, and they always seemed to make his mom feel more comfortable. She called them her "special angels." He remembered how calm and peaceful she looked after the Hospice nurses had visited. But as much as he liked them, remembering those days while his mom was sick still made him feel sad and empty inside.

"I'll think about it, Dad," Johnathan replied. But I knew in my bear heart that he really didn't want to go. ♥

July

Johnathan didn't say anything more about the Hospice camp, and he hoped his dad had forgotten all about it. But Mr. Clarke hadn't forgotten. In fact, he had sent away for more information about it.

"But Dad, do we *have* to go? Why can't we just stay home and be together?"

Mr. Clarke understood why Johnathan felt as he did but answered, "Please trust me on this one, Johnathan. I really think it would be good for both of us. Let's just give it a try, okay?"

During the next week, Mr. Clarke made a list of all the things they'd be packing for their camping trip. Johnathan tried hard to look excited when his dad talked about the soccer games they'd play and the new friends they'd meet. But he didn't *feel* excited, and so he just moped through the days. When he didn't even laugh at my jokes, I knew he needed time to work out his feelings.

The day to leave for camp arrived, and Johnathan looked

pretty miserable as he helped his dad pack their gear into the car. When we were all ready, Johnathan gave me a tight squeeze and whispered, "Come on, Penny Bear. We're in this thing together!"

We rode through the countryside for an hour or so. Finally, Mr. Clarke turned off the highway and drove down a long, narrow dirt road that led to an open area full of parked cars. In a nearby grassy field, a group of kids and adults were playing soccer. As we got out of the car, we were met by two people who said they were from the Hospice camp. They helped us unload the car and then led us along the woodsy path to our cabin. Over the doorway, someone had nailed a hand-painted sign that read, "Welcome, Johnathan and Mr. Clarke."

"Hey, where's *my* name?" I whispered to Johnathan. He laughed at my joke, which I thought was a pretty good sign. Maybe he *was* going to like this place!

We looked around the cabin. It was small and cozy, with bunk beds, a dresser, a small bedside table, and two chairs. Someone had placed a journal on the bedside table, along with a pencil and a bunch of colorful flowers in a tiny basket.

The flowers made Johnathan smile and helped him feel welcome. He plopped his sleeping bag on the top bunk and started to unpack.

Once everything was put away, we headed up the path toward a big wooden building marked "Mess Hall," where we would have our supper and meet the other children and their families. In the food line, Johnathan stood next to a boy his own age named Tommy. While their fathers talked, Tommy introduced himself and asked Johnathan if he and his dad wanted to sit with them. Johnathan smiled. "Yeah, sure." It wasn't long before both of them were talking a mile a minute, just like their dads!

When supper was over, everyone sat outside around the campfire. Each person said their name and the name of their special person who had died. Johnathan was surprised when Tommy said *his* mom had died, too. He leaned against Mr. Clarke and whispered, "Gee, Daddy, I thought I was the only kid in the whole world who didn't have a mom anymore." His dad slipped an arm around him, and Johnathan decided he was glad they had come, because he didn't feel so different or alone anymore.

The weekend seemed to fly by, and Johnathan was disappointed when it was time to leave. While Mr. Clarke loaded our things into the car, Johnathan and I sat together looking out over the lake. He told me his favorite part of the weekend was "memory night." That was when everybody got together and took turns talking about their special person. Johnathan had shown pictures of his mom and told some of his favorite memories, including the one about Valentine's Day and the "happy tears." Then all the campers put pictures of their special loved one up on a big poster. Johnathan was especially pleased when his friend Tommy put his mother's picture right next to the one of Johnathan's mom.

When it was time for Johnathan and Tommy to say goodbye, they gave each other a big bear hug and promised to be e-mail pals. As we drove back down the dirt road, Johnathan waved and waved, until he could no longer see his new friend. With happy tears in his eyes, Johnathan picked me up and held me tightly on his lap. "I'll remember this special place forever, Penny Bear," he whispered.

Now that camp was over, the rest of July seemed to drag. Johnathan could hardly wait for August, because he was going to visit Aunt Sally and Uncle Doug at their farm. ♥

AUGUST

As soon as August arrived, Johnathan kept asking his father how many more days he had to wait until it was time for him to go visit his Aunt Sally and Uncle Doug on their farm. Johnathan wasn't usually such a pest, and he knew how to count the days on the calendar, but he was getting tired of waiting for August 15th. "How many more days until August 15th?" became a frequent question around the house, and each time Mr. Clarke answered, I was amazed at how patient he was with his young son.

I understood why Johnathan was so restless and eager to travel. There wasn't much to do at home. Most of his friends were away on vacation with their families, and although Mrs. Short was there to look after him during the day, Johnathan felt lonely. He felt sad, too, because summer had been such a special time for him and his mom. He told me about some of the fun things they'd do together, like picnic in the woods, take bike rides in the park, swim at the YMCA pool, and climb the hill behind their house to watch the fireworks.

At last, August 15th arrived, and Mr. Clarke didn't even need to ask Johnathan to finish packing, because Johnathan's bags had been packed for weeks!

As we drove along the mountain roads toward his aunt and uncle's farm, Johnathan chattered excitedly, wondering what he'd do first. He said he hoped Uncle Doug would take him fishing on the pond in the little rowboat and then stop near the lily pads where a family of frogs lived. Maybe his Aunt Sally would let him help her bake fresh cornbread.

On the phone, Aunt Sally had told Johnathan that since he was now old enough, he'd be responsible for regular chores on the farm. He'd be in charge of feeding the chickens each morning and collecting their eggs in the afternoon, and he'd help feed and groom the horses in the barn. Johnathan couldn't wait to get there!

Mr. Clarke's car had barely come to a complete stop when Johnathan jumped out and ran to give his aunt and uncle a big hug! Then he introduced me, and Aunt Sally and Uncle Doug gave me a big hug, too. They made me feel so welcome!

The days on the farm were wonderful. Each morning we got up early to the sound of the rooster's "cock-a-doodle-doo." Still dressed in his pajamas, Johnathan would take a flashlight and find his way to the chicken coop, where the hens squawked and pecked hungrily at the feed. Then he'd return to the cozy kitchen for breakfast. Aunt Sally loved to surprise Johnathan with something freshly baked. One morning she served muffins made with the raspberries Johnathan and I had picked just the day before. Another morning she made scrambled eggs with the eggs we had collected from the hens' nests. I could see why Johnathan enjoyed farm life and farm food!

The two-week visit was like a dream come true for Johnathan until one afternoon, when he became kind of cranky. I think he was feeling grumpy because the next day he would be leaving the farm to go back home.

Aunt Sally asked him to go with Uncle Doug to help pick green beans and broccoli. "But I don't even *like* dumb old green beans and broccoli. You're not my mother! You can't tell me what to do!" He took a deep breath and shouted, "I won't *ever* love anyone like I loved my mom!"

Johnathan's cheeks got redder than the raspberries we'd picked, and tears streamed down his face. As soon as the words were out of his mouth, he felt awful about getting mad at his

aunt. He grabbed me from the table and turned to run out the door, but Aunt Sally quickly bent down and wrapped her arms around him.

"It's okay, Johnathan. It's okay," she said softly. "I know you miss your mom a lot. So do I." Johnathan's body was shaking from the anger and tears. "No one can ever replace your wonderful mom. But it's okay to love me for just being your Aunt Sally. You can love different people in different ways. In your heart you will always love your mom in a *very* special way!"

I felt all the anger melt out of Johnathan. He hugged Aunt Sally and said he was really sorry for yelling at her. His words poured out... "I've been so busy here on the farm that I haven't thought about Mom at all. I don't want to forget her. And what about my dad? Who's taking care of *him*?"

These thoughts were very confusing for Johnathan. Aunt Sally listened and answered calmly, "It's okay to just be a kid, Johnathan, and to be busy and have fun. That's exactly what your mom would want for you. And your dad, too. He's taking care of his 'dad stuff,' and he wants you to take care of your 'kid stuff.'"

She smiled and added, "And speaking of dad and kid stuff, why don't you ask Uncle Doug where to find the blueberry bushes at the edge of the woods? If you and Penny Bear can pick a basketful today, I'll show you how to make a blueberry pie. There'll be enough berries left over to make your dad's favorite blueberry pancakes for breakfast when he comes tomorrow."

The thought of the look on his dad's face when he saw fresh blueberry pancakes covered with butter and syrup was enough to send Johnathan racing across the farm to find Uncle Doug. He not only helped his uncle pick green beans and broccoli in the vegetable garden, but he also found the blueberry patch and filled *two* baskets!

As we said our goodbyes the next morning, Johnathan gave Aunt Sally an extra hug. "I really *do* love you, Aunt Sally," he whispered. Then louder he said, "You're the best aunt in the whole, wide world!" Out of the corner of my eye I thought I saw Aunt Sally wink at me. Hmmm... I wonder if she suspects that I'm a magical bear. ♥

SEPTEMBER

September didn't start off very well. School was still more than a week away, and Mr. Clarke seemed worried about Johnathan. I think he noticed how unhappy and quiet his son had been ever since we got back from Aunt Sally's farm. It was time for another bear-to-boy talk. I snuggled over to Johnathan one afternoon as he lay on the couch with his unopened mystery book beside him.

Johnathan sat up and said, "Penny Bear, do you think there's something wrong with me? Nothing seems fun anymore. I feel tired all the time, and I just don't feel like doing anything, not even reading. Do you think I'm sick and I'm going to die like Mom did?"

Because these questions had been bottled up inside of Johnathan, they came pouring out fast. I wasn't quite sure how to answer. So I said, "No, Johnathan, you're not sick. When someone we love dies, it takes a lot of energy from us and it's normal to feel tired. Sometimes the feelings that get stuck inside us can make us feel tired, too."

I took a deep breath and suggested the time was right for him to begin to write regularly in the journal he had brought home from the Hospice camp. "You can write anything you want.... ideas, feelings, questions. You could even write poems or letters to your mom." I reminded him of the "feeling words" he had written on his calendar. "Just write what's in your heart," I added. "Or, how about drawing pictures? Sometimes making a drawing about how we feel can help the hurt go away."

Write From My Heart ♥ Journal
by Johnathan Clarke

He thought about it for a minute, then he grinned and ran upstairs. He came back carrying his Hospice journal and a box of markers. Johnathan wrote across the cover of the journal, "Write from My Heart ♥ Journal by Johnathan Clarke."

I picked it up and said, "Perfect! Remember that this is your private journal and you don't have to show it to anyone. When you write what's on your mind and in your heart, you'll write your true feelings. They can be happy, sad, or even angry — whatever you're feeling at that moment is okay to put in the book."

Johnathan did a lot of writing after that, and I could see how much it helped him. He played with his friends more, had more energy, and seemed happier around the house.

Now the long, hot summer days were over, and school

was about to start. Johnathan and his dad went back-to-school shopping. First, they picked out all his school supplies, and that was fun. But when they went to look at clothes, Johnathan's stomach started to feel funny, like it was tied up in knots. He and his dad had never gone shopping together for clothes before. That was always something his mom did with him.

Everything that his dad picked out, Johnathan didn't like. And everything that Johnathan held up, his dad frowned at it and said he wasn't sure it was the right size or color. Johnathan was close to tears, and Mr. Clarke was getting annoyed. They needed a break. Maybe if one of them would just admit why they were having such a hard time clothes shopping, they could laugh or cry about it, I thought to myself.

It was as though Mr. Clarke had read my mind. In the dressing room, as he helped Johnathan pull a blue-and-white striped jersey over his head, Mr. Clarke said, "Sorry, Johnathan, I guess I'm not a very good clothes shopper. You know Mom was the clothes shopper in the family." He hesitated a second, then continued, "You want to know a secret?"

Johnathan popped his head through the neck opening of the jersey. He was all ears. "You might not believe this, but Mom used to buy all my clothes, too. She knew I didn't like shopping, so whenever I needed socks or shirts or pants — or even shoes — she'd ask if she could get them for me."

Johnathan grinned. "And you always said yes, right, Dad?"

Mr. Clarke nodded. Then Johnathan whispered, "I won't tell anyone. I promise. It will be just our secret." And then they *both* grinned.

After that, Johnathan and his dad became a great shopping team. They quickly picked out five new shirts, three pairs of pants, and a jacket. It was great to see both of them heading for the cashier's desk with big smiles on their faces.

Johnathan's new clothes were packed into a shopping bag with handles. He let me ride in the bag while he and his dad walked to the shoe store. Once we got there, Johnathan grabbed me and raced over to an empty seat, where he stood me up and measured my bear feet with a big, sliding metal ruler.

"Hi, Johnathan, it's good to see you," said Mr. Dugan, the shoe store owner. "Time for new school shoes? Is it just you and your teddy bear shopping today?"

"Nope. I'm here with my dad," Johnathan said as Mr. Clarke caught up with us.

"Nice to meet you, Mr. Clarke. Where's Mrs. Clarke today?"

Johnathan's eyes darted up to his dad's face. Everything went silent. Mr. Clarke cleared his throat and answered, "My wife died in January."

Johnathan didn't want to listen to Mr. Dugan say how sorry he was. He just wanted to get out of that store! When Mr. Clarke saw how tightly Johnathan was holding on to me, he said, "I think we'll come back later. Johnathan and I are kind of all shopped out for today." Reaching for the shopping bag with one hand and giving Johnathan's shoulder a little squeeze with the other, Mr. Clarke thanked Mr. Dugan for understanding and led us out of the store. I whispered to Johnathan that I was glad his dad handled things in such a brave way. I could tell by the look of relief on Johnathan's face that he agreed.

When the first day of school came, Johnathan told me he had that funny feeling in his stomach again. He was worried about whether he'd like the new teacher, about how many of his classmates he would know, and if the new kids would think he was weird because he didn't have a mother. And that was just the beginning! He must have asked a hundred "what if" questions, until finally he stuffed me into his new backpack and we headed out the door.

When he met the other kids in the schoolyard, Johnathan could tell right away they were happy to see him. Worrying so much had used up a lot of his energy, but everything went just fine. He even liked the new teacher a lot, and he told me he couldn't wait to go back the next day! ♥

OCTOBER

The days got a little cooler, the leaves began to change colors, and people started putting up Halloween decorations. Johnathan and Mr. Clarke carved out a pumpkin that had one half of its face smiling and the other half looking scary. They placed it in the big front window.

When we woke up Halloween morning, Johnathan said, "I can't decide what I want to be for Halloween, Penny Bear. Last year Mom made me this really cool costume — even my dad didn't recognize me! Maybe I'll just wear that one again."

I nodded encouragingly.

That afternoon, Johnathan dragged the Halloween costume out of his closet to show me. He struggled to put it on, but got stuck and started to cry with frustration. "It's too *small*, Penny Bear," he cried, wiggling out of the costume and throwing it on the floor. "Oh forget Halloween, anyway. It's a dumb holiday!" With that, he grabbed me, climbed onto his bed, and pulled the quilt over our heads.

Mr. Clarke knocked at the bedroom door. "May I come

in, Johnathan?" From under the covers, Johnathan answered with a weak "Okay." I peeked out from under the quilt and saw how surprised Johnathan's dad looked to find him in bed. Mr. Clarke picked up the pieces of the costume. Then he looked at the two bumps we made under the covers, and came over and sat down by the bigger bump.

"Do you want to talk about Halloween, Johnathan?" he asked.

Johnathan pulled me back in closer to him. "My stomach hurts, my costume doesn't fit, and nothing's the same anymore. Everything stinks."

Mr. Clarke was quiet for a few moments, then he said, "You know, Johnathan, I was thinking the same thing today, that nothing seems to work for me, either. I'm even having a hard time putting the bags of candy together for the trick-or-treaters. Maybe this year we could both just stay home and give out the candy together. What do you think about that idea?

Johnathan pulled off the quilt. "That's a great idea, Dad," he said. "Wait a minute — why are you smiling like that? You're up to something, Dad. I just know it! Tell me!"

Mr. Clarke grinned. "I had another idea. Remember my telling you that every Halloween my dad and I would make a scarecrow? And when I got to be about your age, I asked him why they were called scarecrows when they really never did scare anyone, especially the crows!"

Johnathan nodded, and jumped off the bed. He guessed where his dad was going with this.

"Yesss! Let's make a scarecrow, Dad! We have that old broom handle in the garage, and there's that bale of hay Aunt Sally and Uncle Doug brought the last time they came."

They worked the rest of the afternoon creating a terrific scarecrow. They had just settled it in the perfect spot in the front yard when a big crow came circling overhead. The crow looked down at Johnathan, at Mr. Clarke, and at the scarecrow. Then it landed smack dab on top of the scarecrow's floppy hat.

Johnathan and his dad burst out laughing. They laughed so hard they had to sit down. Then they got up on wobbly legs and went inside to fix goodie bags for the trick-or-treaters. Later they had fun answering the doorbell and pretending to be frightened by the scary costumes. And they made sure they told all the kids how great they looked, just like Johnathan's mom always did every year when she handed out treats.

So it turned out to be a fun-filled Halloween after all, filled with big laughs and giggly silliness. My bear heart was as happy as could be. ♥

NOVEMBER

Johnathan and his dad were invited to his Aunt Sue and Uncle Giff's house for Thanksgiving. He was really looking forward to seeing his grandparents, aunts and uncles, and some of the cousins he hadn't seen since the day of his mom's funeral.

It sounded as though everybody was already there when we arrived on Thanksgiving morning. As Mr. Clarke knocked on the door, we could hear laughing and could even smell the turkey cooking. Johnathan hugged me close and I could feel how fast his heart was beating. He was excited to see everyone, and happy to be getting so many hugs, but he whispered to me a little later how strange it felt to be at a family gathering without his mom.

While everyone was settling around the table for dinner, Johnathan slid me under his chair. All the food smelled delicious, but I had one of my "bear feelings" that something was missing. Something didn't feel right.

With all the conversations going on, not one person ever

mentioned Johnathan's mom. It almost seemed as if the others had decided earlier in the day not to talk about her in front of Johnathan and his dad because they were afraid it might upset them.

Johnathan's grandfather tapped his glass with his spoon to get everyone's attention and announced, "All right, everyone. It's time for each of us to tell what we're thankful for this Thanksgiving. We'll go right around the table."

Johnathan was relieved to see that he would be the last to speak. Waiting for his turn gave him a chance to think. As each person spoke, Johnathan's heart beat faster and faster. My "bear senses" told me that he didn't know what to feel thankful for. After all, this was the year his mom had died. I thought he could use some support, so I tugged at his pant leg to get his attention. He ignored me, though, so I figured he had a plan of his own.

When it was his turn to speak, Johnathan said, "I'm thankful for my dad *and* (as he picked me up from the floor) for my Penny Bear." Everyone laughed and I knew this was my chance! "Talk about your mom right now!" I whispered to him. "It's okay... it's good!"

Johnathan swallowed hard and said, "I'm also thankful for my mom." Everyone suddenly became very quiet. Johnathan hugged me and continued, "I'm thankful for all the great memories I have of her." Still no one spoke, and Johnathan noticed that his grandmother had tears on her cheeks. He thought that maybe he'd done the wrong thing.

Just then his grandfather spoke up. "Speaking of memories, Johnathan, I'll never forget that Thanksgiving at your house when you and I were in charge of taking your mother's famous apple pie to the dining room." His grandfather looked around at the others. "See, as I was taking the pie out of the oven, I turned and bumped smack into Johnathan and dropped the pie all over the counter. What a mess! Johnathan, you suggested we scoop it up and put it in a bowl. You said that no one would even notice. So, that's what we did! Then we carried it out to the table and set it in front of your mom.

"She looked really shocked at first, but she took a deep breath and announced that it was a new mystery dessert! She hid it under lots of ice cream and saved the day."

At this point, everyone was laughing. Johnathan's dad said, "I never knew until this very moment what the real story was behind that mystery dessert!" That seemed to break the ice, and the others joined in with "remember-when" stories of their own.

I was so proud of Johnathan! If anyone had thought to ask *me* what I was thankful for, I would have said, without a doubt, that it was having Johnathan as my best friend. I was so happy to be part of this wonderful family on Thanksgiving Day! ♥

DECEMBER

The holiday season was in full swing. Stores, houses, and streets everywhere were brightly decorated, and everyone seemed excited and full of happy spirit. But Johnathan couldn't feel the magic. He told me in one of our boy-to-bear talks that his class at school had been discussing all the ways people of the world celebrate their holiday customs. Johnathan said that Christmas had always been his favorite time of year — until now.

"Johnathan, your mom would want you to feel all the love and happiness that comes with Christmas," I told him as we sat side by side on his bed.

Johnathan thought about what I said, and slowly a smile appeared on his face. He had an idea! Johnathan jumped up and disappeared into his closet. He returned carrying boxes that had the words, "Johnathan's Private Christmas Decorations," written on them in crayon. As he opened each box, Johnathan smiled and laughed.

"Look at this angel, Penny Bear. I made it when I was

only four years old!"

We had fun decorating the whole room with colored lights and all his handmade decorations. Johnathan had just finished putting the angel on top of a little tree when Mr. Clarke knocked on the door. Johnathan called out, "Wait a minute, Dad, we have a surprise for you!" He turned off his lamp and turned on the Christmas lights.

"Okay, Dad, come in!"

Mr. Clarke's face lit up as he exclaimed, "Wow! Johnathan, this looks great! I'm so proud of you, and you did it all by yourself!" Then he quickly added, "with Penny Bear's help, no doubt!"

When Johnathan turned his lamp back on, he noticed that his dad was holding a big box that had a sticker with the words, "Open Before Christmas." He was curious. "What's in the box, Dad?"

Mr. Clarke put his arm around Johnathan and said, "I have a special surprise for you, too."

I watched Johnathan excitedly open the box. As he pushed aside the tissue paper, he picked up an envelope and then became very quiet. Tears rolled down his cheeks when he saw the words, "For my Johnathan..." written in his mom's handwriting. He slowly opened the envelope.

A faint smell of lavender filled the room as Johnathan began to read the letter from his mom:

> Dearest Johnathan,
>
> In some ways, this is the hardest letter I have ever had to write, yet in other ways, it is the easiest. Remember when I told you about 'happy tears?' Well, my cheeks are so sparkly from happy tears that I am glowing!
>
> Dad is sitting on the bed next to me as I write this, and his face is sparkling, too. We must look like two of the brightest stars you would ever hope to see in the sky. Or maybe our sparkly faces look more like shiny lights on a Christmas tree!
>
> Before you open the package Dad has given you, I want to tell you a secret.
>
> When Dad and I learned that I had just a short time to live, we asked the volunteers who provide Penny Bears to visit us here at the house so we could pick out a Penny Bear for you.
>
> I'll never forget the day we chose your Penny Bear. Lined up at the foot of my bed were twelve of the cutest bears we had ever seen! Dad and I were having a hard time choosing the right one for you. We

were telling the Penny Bear volunteers that we wanted your bear to be an extra special friend — a friend you can tell your fears to, cuddle and cry with, and laugh with, too.

As I was about to finish my sentence, the bear with the striped sweater tumbled off the bed! I reached down to pick him up and saw that he had landed upside down, with his head stuck in my slipper!

Imagine how silly he looked wearing a fuzzy pink slipper as a hat! We all got the giggles, and Dad and I knew that <u>this</u> was the Penny Bear for you!

Later that day, as I sat holding your bear, I had a wonderful idea for a Christmas present for you. You'll see what I mean when you open the package, which I'd like you to do before you turn the page and read the rest of my letter.

Johnathan gently placed the letter aside, then unwrapped the package. Inside were matching sweaters, one for Johnathan, and one for me. Each sweater had a little rainbow heart pocket on it with a shiny new penny tucked inside.

Johnathan pulled his on, then dressed me in mine. "It's like Mom sent us a hug, Penny Bear," he said softly. Blinking back tears, Johnathan picked up his mom's letter and continued reading:

> *My sweet Johnathan, I had such fun making these sweaters for you and Penny Bear. You know how much I always enjoyed knitting. Well, working on a project that I knew would make you happy made me feel happy, even on days when I was feeling sad.*
>
> *Every time you see or touch the heart-shaped rainbow pocket on your sweater, I want you to remember that the precious love we have for each other will always shine brightly — just like the beautiful colors of the rainbow.*
>
> *I have always been so proud of you, Johnathan. I love you dearly... and always will.*
>
> *Love, hugs, and kisses,*
> *Mom*

Mr. Clarke and Johnathan hugged tightly, then they gave *me* a big hug. I saw sparkly tears on their faces, and I knew that Johnathan was once again feeling the magic of the holiday season. ♥

A New Year Begins...

In January, there was plenty of fresh, dry snow — perfect for sledding. One cold but sunny day, Johnathan pulled me on his new sled up to the hill behind his house. After lots of rides down the slope with me sitting in his lap, Johnathan and I sat on a big rock at the top to rest.

"You know, Penny Bear, the last time I went sledding, I was with Mom," Johnathan said in a low voice. "It's hard to believe a whole year has gone by since she died."

Johnathan was holding me tightly, and I could feel how fast his heart was beating. "Penny Bear, I still wonder if Mom's okay. Is it nice where she is? Will my stomach ever stop hurting when I get 'reminders' about her? Are you sure she'll always remember me and love me like she said in my Christmas letter?"

Johnathan had so many questions! He told me sometimes he felt dumb asking them, but I assured him that it was only dumb when you *don't* ask!

"Everyone hopes for answers to help them understand

things more easily, Johnathan," I said. "There are some questions that even grownups can't answer. And remember what it said on my tag: It's okay not to have all the answers. Some will come in time, but some will always remain a mystery. What I do know is how proud of you I am, and that it's an honor to be your friend!"

I told Johnathan I was proud of him because of all he learned during his year of feeling sad and missing his mom, which was called "grief." When he was afraid or had angry feelings, he learned how to ask questions, write in his journal, and turn sad reminders into happy memories.

"Johnathan, you have learned how important it is to trust yourself and others. You have been very brave to let your teachers, family, and friends help you with your sadness."

As we continued to sit on the hillside, we saw the sky start to brighten and change colors. "Look, Penny Bear, it's a *rainbow!*" cried Johnathan, his eyes wide with surprise. "I've never seen a rainbow in winter. Isn't it beautiful? It's the same as the little heart pockets on our sweaters that Mom made us. And it kind of looks like the rainbow our kites made on my birthday."

With tears in his eyes, Johnathan whispered, "Penny Bear, I know — I just *know* — that Mom painted that rainbow for me!" I felt sad watching the tears run down his face. Johnathan quickly said, "No, Penny Bear, it's all right. I feel different this time, remembering Mom. Look, these are *happy* tears —

they're the sparkle kind!"

Then Johnathan said, "Even though I miss my mom so much, Penny Bear, I know she's okay and I will be, too. Rainbows will always remind me that Mom loves me and that she will be in my heart forever." ♥

Well, my friend, we have come to the end of our story... and now there is a new beginning for Johnathan. I came into Johnathan's life when he most needed a friend to help him understand that the love and memories we share with someone special never end. May you feel the comfort and joy of love — the greatest gift of all.

From my heart to yours,
Penny Bear ♥

THANK YOU HUGS

I have been blessed by many people who believed in my purpose for writing *Penny Bear's Gift of Love*. It would take another book to thank them all individually, and they know only too well how long it took to write *this* one! Please know how much I love and appreciate you, and that I thank you from the bottom of my heart for believing in this story and in our Penny Bears.

Writing a book is not an easy undertaking. I am grateful for the love, energy and creative talents shared by my dear friends: Elissa Al-Chokhachy; Sally Ballard; Elizabeth Byrne Dawes; Jan Carlton Doetsch; Michiko Eager; Mark May, in memory of his little daughter, Chanel; The Mills family (Ellen, Reagan, and Danny), in memory of their husband and father, Lenny; Christina Sweetland; Merry Tufts and her son Roger, and our Editor Karla Wheeler. Karla's daughter, Jenny, drew the bear illustration for the Father's Day picnic invitation.

Thank you All so much!

And finally, I wish to thank my friend Marilyn Freeman – an earth angel – who has been the wind beneath my wings. Marilyn has put her heart and soul into this book and The Penny Bear Company. I will be forever grateful for her encouragement, talent, long hours of writing and rewriting, but most of all, her beautiful friendship!

My wish in writing *Penny Bear's Gift of Love* is that whoever walks the path of grief will be touched and reassured by the messages of hope we've tried to offer. When the way is lonely, please know that there are others who have walked there, too, who will turn and light the way with understanding and kindness. And there you will find a hand waiting to hold yours…

With love and light,

Penny ♥

ABOUT THE AUTHOR

*Penny Wigglesworth
with her huggable
"Penny Bears."*

PENNY WIGGLESWORTH is the founder of the The Penny Bear Company, a non-profit, all-volunteer organization based in Marblehead, Massachusetts.

The Penny Bear Company began as the result of a bee sting Penny experienced on a golf course, her near-fatal allergic reaction to it, and the "coincidence" of having an allergist nearby who saved her life.

After this near-death incident, Penny no longer feared death. She realized how quickly life can be over and that we should enjoy every minute of each day. She knew she needed to work with those who were dying and those who loved them.

Penny completed a ten-week training program with a local Hospice organization. As a volunteer, she met 16-year-old Seth Bailey, who was diagnosed with leukemia at age three. As mentioned in "A Welcome Hug" at the beginning of the book, The Penny Bear Company was an outgrowth of Seth's search for a purpose in life and a way to help others.

"Penny Bears," as they are affectionately called, are named not for Penny Wigglesworth, but rather for the message found on each U.S. penny: "In God We Trust." Each Penny Bear wears a sweater knitted by dedicated volunteers. Tucked inside the rainbow pocket on each sweater is a shiny new penny, which serves as a reminder of the importance of faith and hope in our lives.

The charitable outreach of The Penny Bear Company extends far and wide, bringing hugs wherever they are needed. Be sure to visit **www.pennybear.org** to learn more.

ABOUT THE ILLUSTRATOR

*Michiko Eager
with her sons,
Michael and Matthew.*

As a child in Yokohama, Japan, MICHIKO EAGER dreamed of one day illustrating children's books. Michiko was new to America when she was first introduced to our Penny Bear volunteers. Her life's dreams and natural artistic talents connected instantly with the loving outreach mission of The Penny Bear Company.

Michiko is now a resident of New Hampshire, where she is balancing her artwork career with her role as the mother of two young boys.

Bear facts

HOW TO ORDER
BOOKS AND BEARS

♥   By Mail: The Penny Bear™ Company, Inc.
Six Elmwood Road
Marblehead, MA 01945

♥   By Phone: (781) 639-2828

♥   By Email: bear@pennybear.org

Please be sure to visit our website to learn more about our
non-profit, all-volunteer organization:

www.pennybear.org